CW00727779

AVENGERS INFINITY WAR: SUPER HERO SKETCH BOOK
A CENTUM BOOK 9781911461814
Published in Great Britain by Centum Books Ltd
This edition published 2018
1 3 5 7 9 10 8 6 4 2

© 2018 MARVEL

All rights reserved. No part of this publication may be reproduced, stored in a retrieval system, or transmitted in any form or by any means, electronic, mechanical, photocopying, recording or otherwise, without the prior permission of the publishers.

Centum Books Ltd, 20 Devon Square, Newton Abbot, Devon, TQ12 2HR, UK
books@centumbooksltd.co.uk

CENTUM BOOKS Limited Reg. No. 07641486

A CIP catalogue record for this book is available from the British Library

Printed in China

MARVEL

AVENGERS
INFINITY WAR

SUPER HERO
SKETCH
BOOK

centum

THANOS

WILL STOP AT NOTHING TO COLLECT ALL SIX INFINITY STONES.

ADD the GOLDEN INFINITY GAUNTLET to his arm.

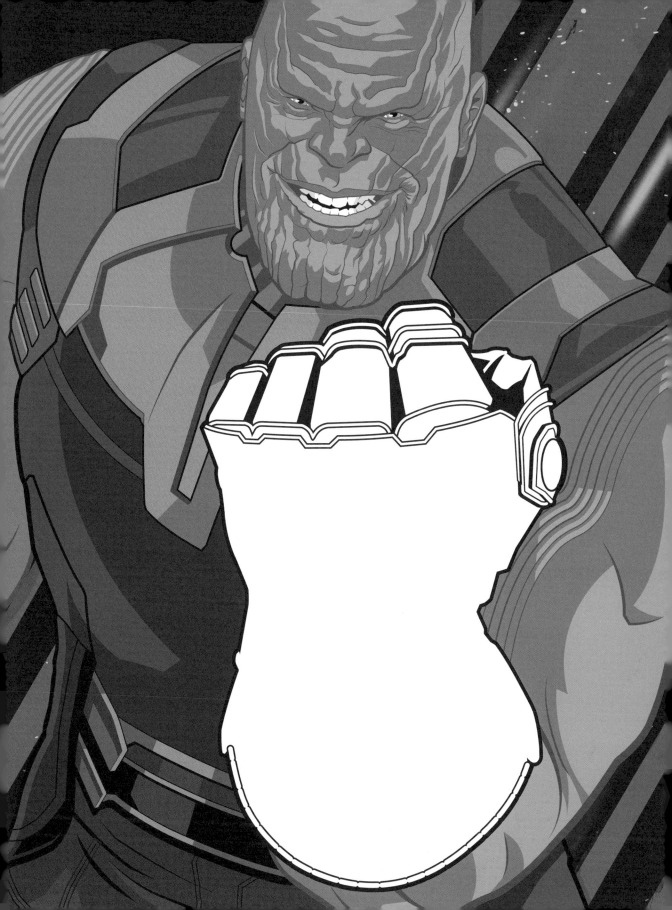

DRAW A SCENE OF DVASTATION BEHIND HIM.

THE MIND STONE IN VISION'S HEAD
IS A VERY POWERFUL WEAPON.

THOR IS THE GOD OF THUNDER.

FILL THE PAGE WITH FLASHES OF LIGHTNING.

USUALLY CLEAN-CUT CAPTAIN AMERICA HAS GROWN A BEARD.

DRAW YOURSELF WITH A **BIG BUSHY BEARD,** and maybe a moustache!

THIS GENERAL OUTRIDER IS READY FOR HIS NEXT MISSION.

SKETCH A WHOLE ARMY OF OUTRIDERS STANDING BEHIND HIM.

IRON SPIDER has been practising his WEB-SLINGING skills.

COVER the page in **LOTS** AND **LOTS** of sticky webs.

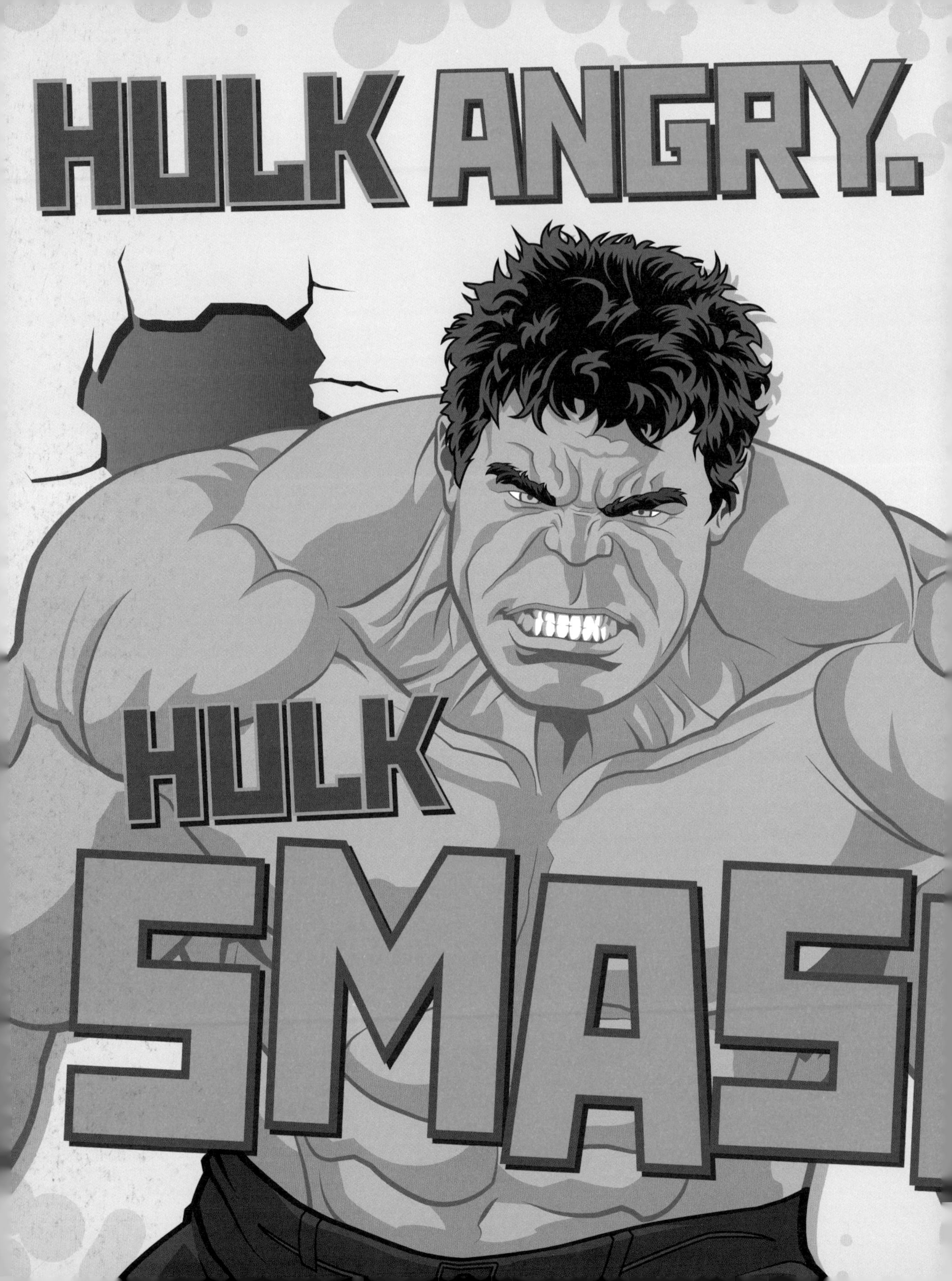
HULK ANGRY.
HULK
SMAS

WHAT'S GOT THE BIG GUY SO STEAMED UP?

DOCTOR STRANGE HAS ACTIVATED THE EYE OF AGAMOTTO.

DRAW THE POWERFUL RELIC AS IT BEGINS TO GROW AND GLOW.

BLACK PANTHER'S SUIT

IS EMBELLISHED WITH AWESOME WAKANDAN PATTERNS.

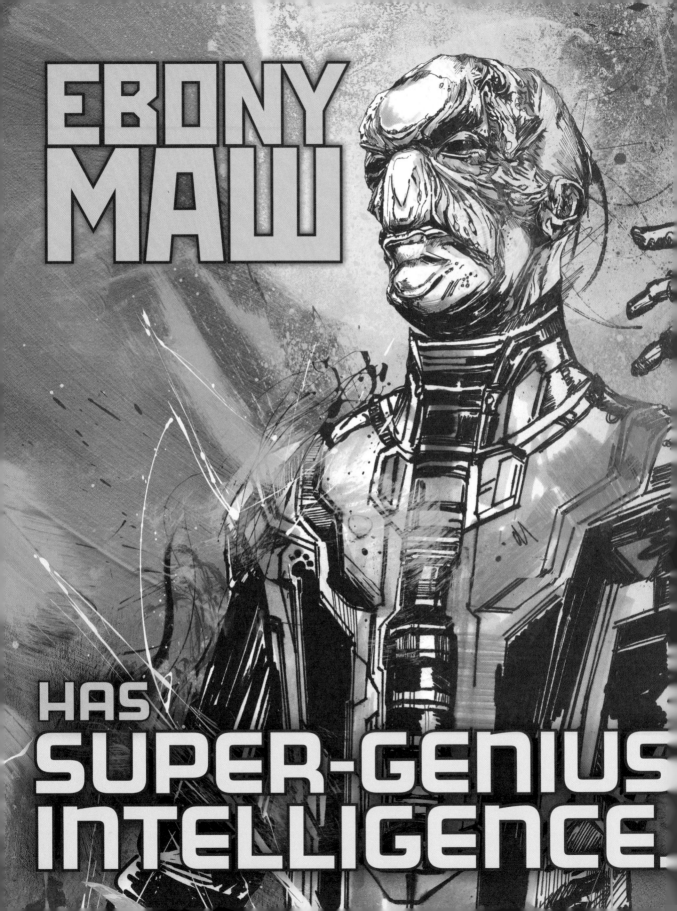

DRAW one of his battle strategies.

BLACK WIDOW

IS A SUPER SPY, AND SHE'S GOT HER LATEST TARGET.

WHO IS SHE WATCHING AND WHY?

IRON MAN AND WAR MACHINE

ARE PATROLLING THE SKIES, SIDE-BY-SIDE.

SKETCH THE SCENE BESIDE THEM.

CULL OBSIDIAN IS HUGE.

DRAW THE ONLY AVENGER WHO CAN MATCH HIM IN SIZE — HULK!

ROCKET IS CERTAIN HE CAN STOP THANOS SINGLE-HANDEDLY.

DOODLE THE GADGET HE'S DESIGNED TO DO THE JOB.

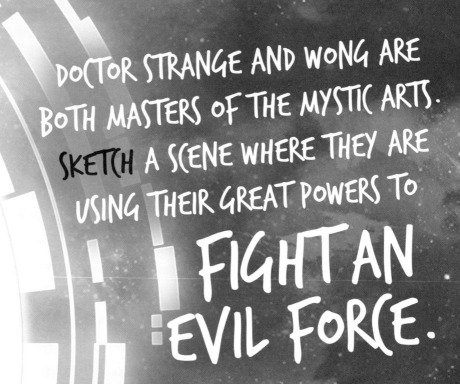

DOCTOR STRANGE AND WONG ARE BOTH MASTERS OF THE MYSTIC ARTS. SKETCH A SCENE WHERE THEY ARE USING THEIR GREAT POWERS TO

FIGHT AN EVIL FORCE.

CORVUS GLAIVE

IS THANOS'S RIGHT-HAND MAN.

DRAW THE PERSON WHO ALWAYS HAS YOUR BACK.

THE AVENGERS WILL HUNT THANOS ACROSS THE GALAXY.

HELP THEM BY DESIGNING A
WANTED POSTER
FOR THE VILLAIN.

WANTED

NAME

PHYSICAL TRAITS

WANTED FOR

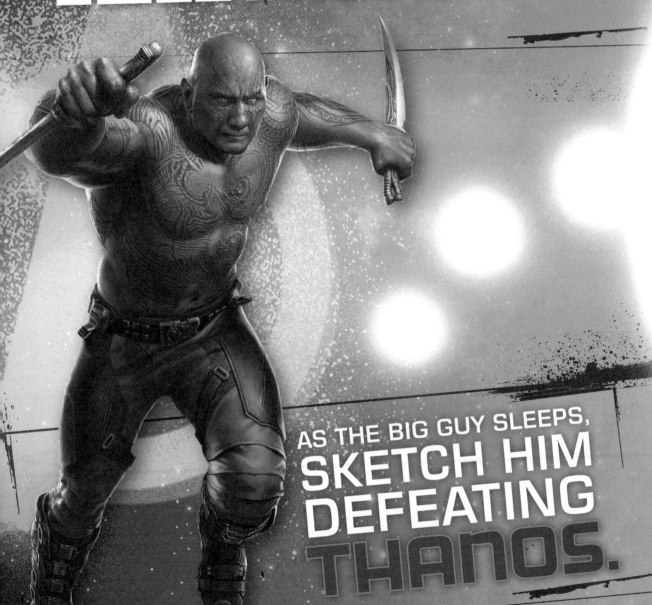

DRAX HAS BEEN DREAMING OF **SWEET REVENGE.**

AS THE BIG GUY SLEEPS, **SKETCH HIM DEFEATING THANOS.**

WHO OR WHAT

HAS JOINED FALCON

FOR A JOYRIDE THROUGH THE CLOUDS?

SKETCH A SCENE OF **TOTAL CHAOS,** AS CONJURED UP BY SCARLET WITCH.

THE INFINITY STONES COULD BE
ANYWHERE!

FILL THE PAGE WITH PLANETS THAT THANOS WILL NEED TO SEARCH.

GAMORA'S SWORD IS ALWAYS SHARP.

SKETCH A VILLAIN FOR HER TO TAKE A SWIPE AT.

FILL THE PAGE WITH OBJECTS THAT ARE AS PURPLE AS **THANOS**.

BLACK PANTHER'S DARK SUIT HELPS HIM BLEND INTO THE SHADOWS

MAKE HIM DISAPPEAR BY COLOURING THE WHOLE PAGE BLACK.

If you were an UNDERCOVER OPERATIVE like BLACK WIDOW, what would YOU need in your SPY KIT?

TOGETHER, THE AVENGERS, THE GUARDIANS, DOCTOR STRANGE AND IRON SPIDER MAKE THE ULTIMATE TEAM.

NAME:

- - - - - - - - -

NAME:

- - - - - - - - -

NAME:

NAME:

NAME:

PICK SOME PALS TO CREATE YOUR OWN SQUAD.

MANTIS IS A POWERFUL EMPATH.

DRAW SOMETHING TO SHOW HER HOW YOU'RE FEELING TODAY.

SUPER-TALENTED WITH A SPEAR,

OKOYE

CAN HIT A BULLS-EYE FROM A GREAT DISTANCE.

TEST HER SKILLS
BY DRAWING SOME
TOUGH TARGETS.

THE GUARDIANS
ARE HAPPY TO HELP
THE AVENGERS
HUNT THANOS.

SKETCH THEIR SHIP
SO THEY'RE READY TO SAIL.

CAPTAIN AMERICA

HAS GONE UNDERGROUND, SO TO CONTACT HIM YOU'LL NEED TO SEND A <u>CODED MESSAGE.</u>

CREATE ONE HERE!

CORVUS' WEAPON IS CALLED A HALBERD.

FILL THIS PAGE WITH OTHER WEAPONS HE COULD USE.

DRAW THE
WIRES THAT
RUN RIGHT
THROUGH HER
ROBOTIC BODY.

CODE NAME:

THE AVENGERS NEED YOU TO HELP TRACK DOWN THANOS!

CREATE YOUR OWN SUPERHERO IDENTITY HERE,
WITH A COOL COSTUME AND CODE NAME.

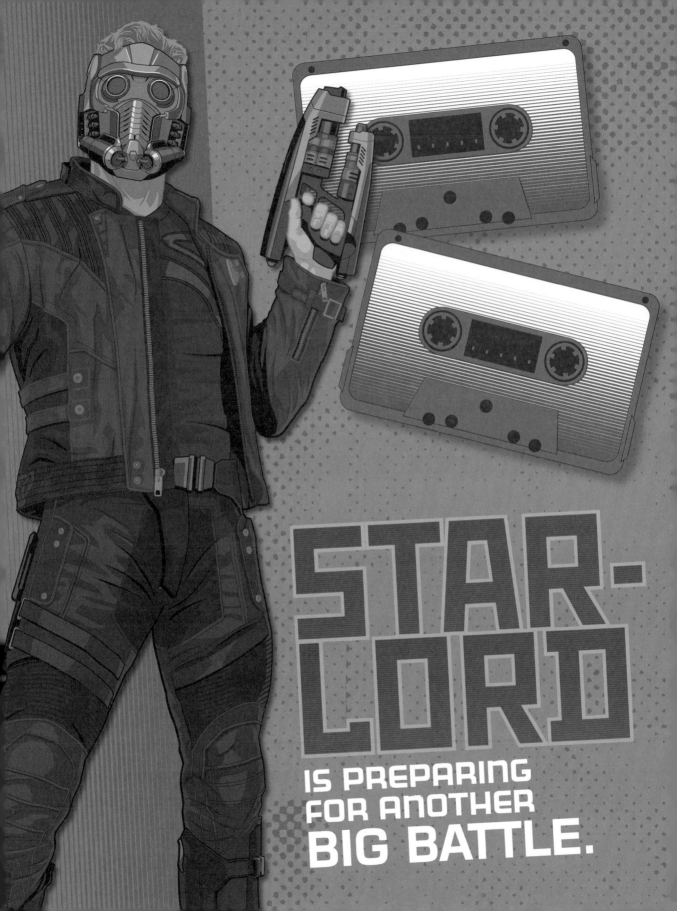

STAR-LORD

IS PREPARING FOR ANOTHER BIG BATTLE.

1

2

3

4

5

6

7

8

9

10

CREATE THE ULTIMATE PLAYLIST TO HELP HIM DEFEAT THANOS.

PROXIMA MIDNIGHT IS AN AMAZING WARRIOR.

SKETCH A NIGHT-TIME SCENE AROUND HER, WITH A FULL MOON AND MANY STARS.

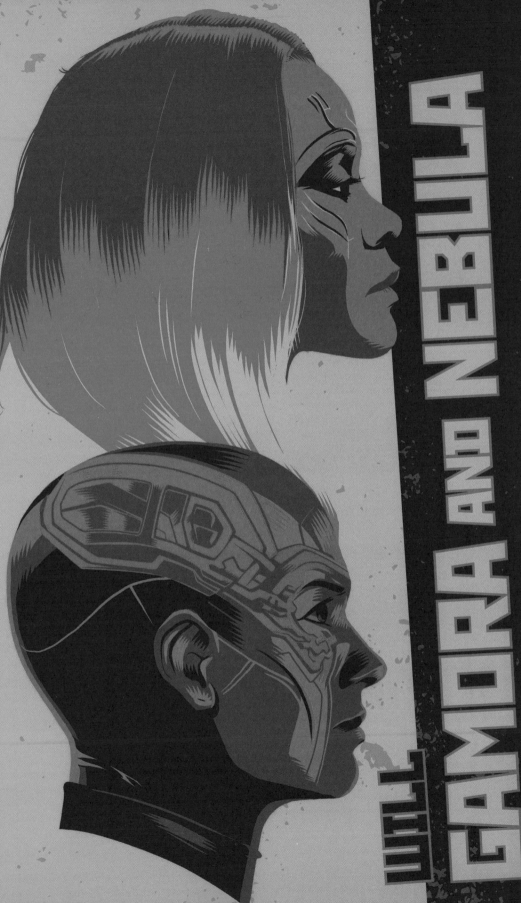

WILL **GAMORA** AND **NEBULA** have the strength to stand up to their father, THANOS?

DRAW THE SISTERS
TEAMING UP AGAINST
THANOS.

WANDA

IS PRACTISING HER TELEKINETIC SKILLS.

HELP THE SCARLET WITCH BY FILLING THE PAGE WITH **GLOWING** HEX SPHERES.

DARK SORCERY IS ONE OF EBONY MAW'S MANY SKILLS.

DOODLE THE SUPER-SCARY SIGHT HE'S CONJURED UP.

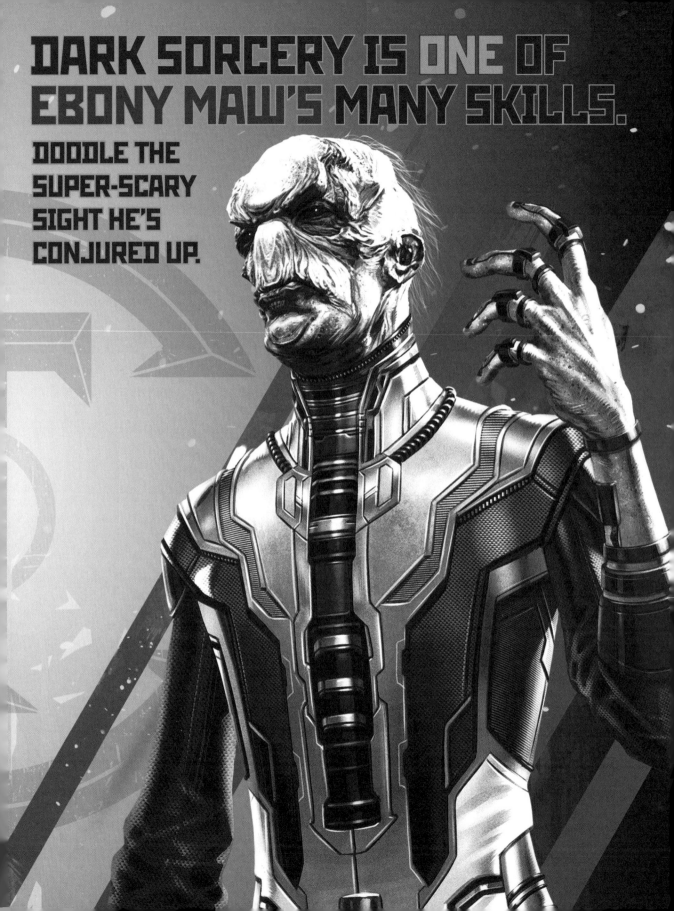

GIVE **WINTER SOLDIER** THE VERY LATEST MECHANICAL **ARM** TO MAKE SURE HE'S READY FOR BATTLE.

CORVUS GLAIVE

IS NEVER WITHOUT HIS
HALBERD.

SKETCH THE SCARY WEAPON,
SO HE'S READY TO SLICE AND DICE.

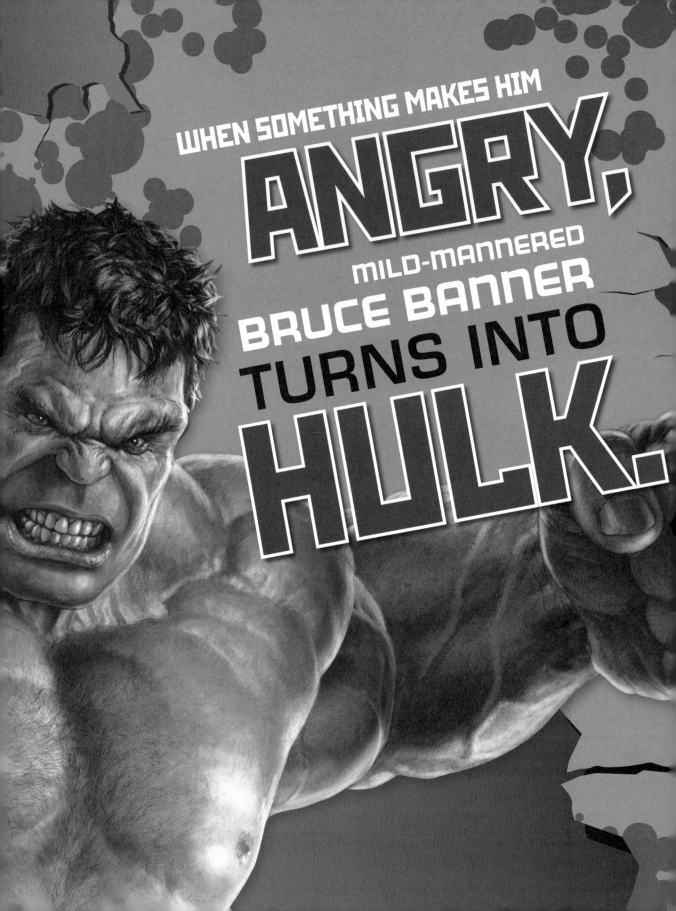

WHEN SOMETHING MAKES HIM **ANGRY,** MILD-MANNERED **BRUCE BANNER** TURNS INTO **HULK.**

LIST THE THINGS THAT MAKE YOU FEEL CROSS.

1

2

3

4

5

6

7

8

SKETCH THE REST OF THE AVENGERS STANDING BEHIND THOR.

ANGRY

HAPPY

SAD

WORK WITH MANTIS TO DRAW OR WRITE DOWN SOMETHING THAT MAKES YOU FEEL EACH OF THESE EMOTIONS.

JEALOUS

SCARED

SURPRISED

WINTER SOLDIER AND CAP

ALWAYS HAVE EACH OTHER'S BACK.

DRAW AN **EPIC** BATTLE SCENE WITH THE BUDDIES FIGHTING **SIDE BY SIDE**.

SSSH!

TONY STARK HAS A NEW INVENTION TO STOP THANOS.

DRAW AND NAME THE TOP-SECRET TECH.

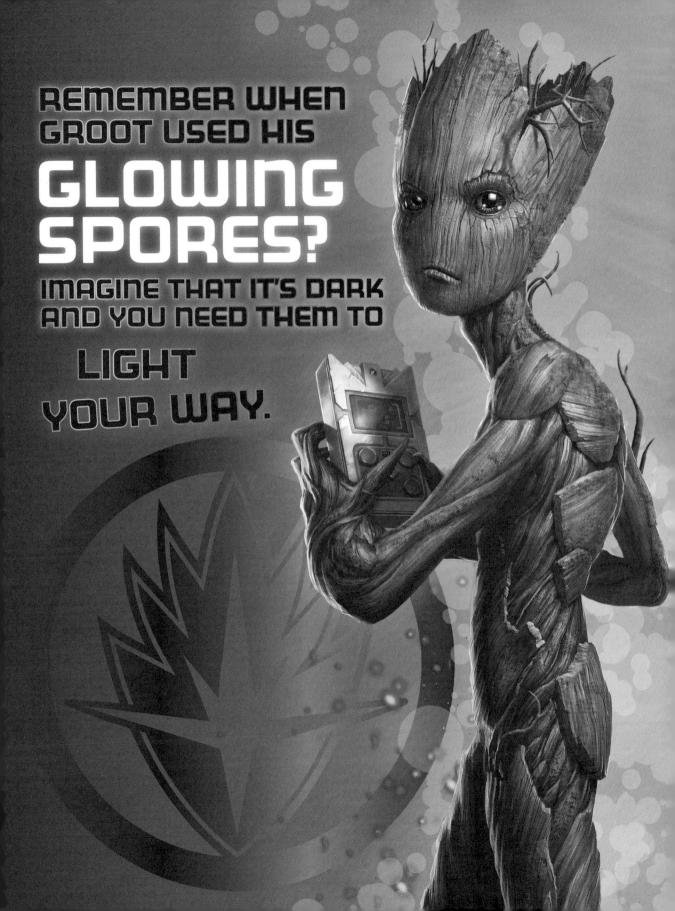

REMEMBER WHEN GROOT USED HIS **GLOWING SPORES?** IMAGINE THAT IT'S DARK AND YOU NEED THEM TO **LIGHT YOUR WAY.**

FILL THE PAGE WITH HIS

LITTLE

FLOATING

LIGHTS.

WHO IS YOUR FAVOURITE MEMBER OF THE AVENGERS?

DRAW THEM HERE, IN AN AWESOME ACTION POSE.

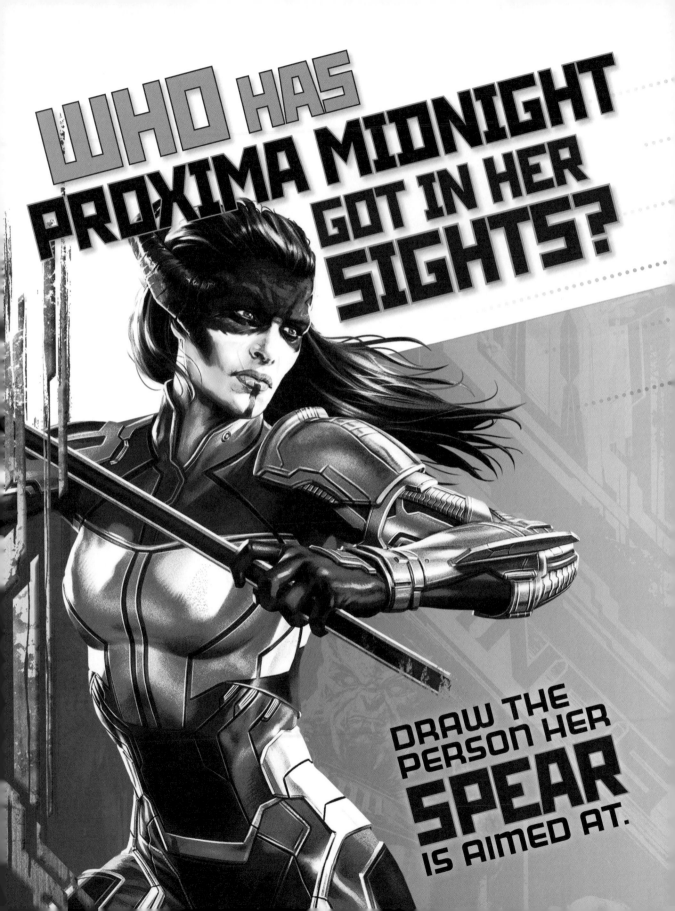

DRAW THE SIX INFINITY STONES

IN THIS SCENE. FOR THANOS TO FIND.

VISION

HAS THE ABILITY TO **PHASE** THROUGH SOLID OBJECTS. SKETCH SOMETHING TO TEST HIS INTANGIBILITY SKILLS.

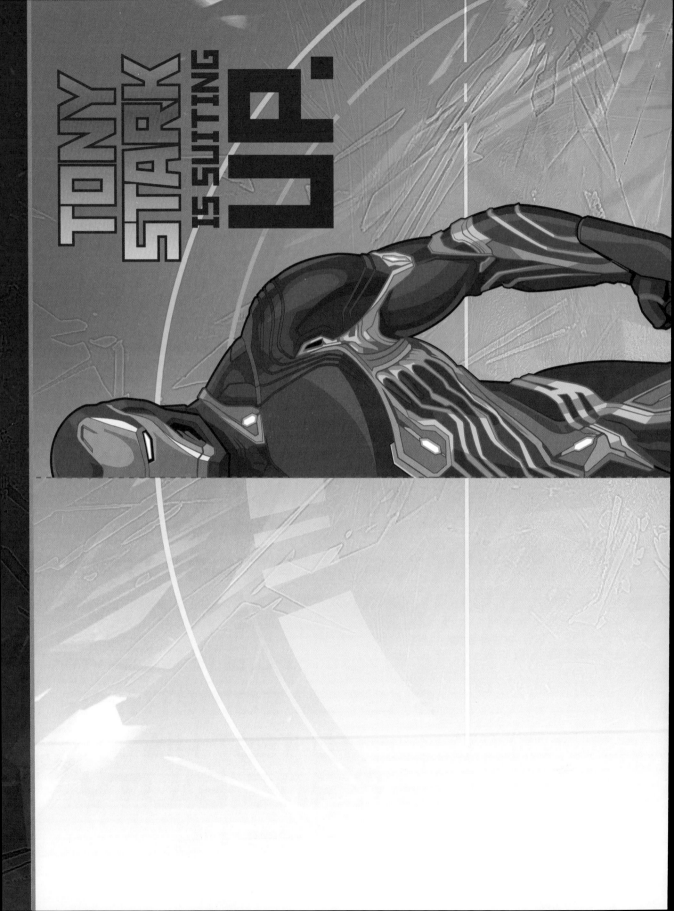

DRAW the other half of his IRON MAN SUIT so he's

READY TO FLY.

WHEN SOMETHING'S OUT OF REACH,

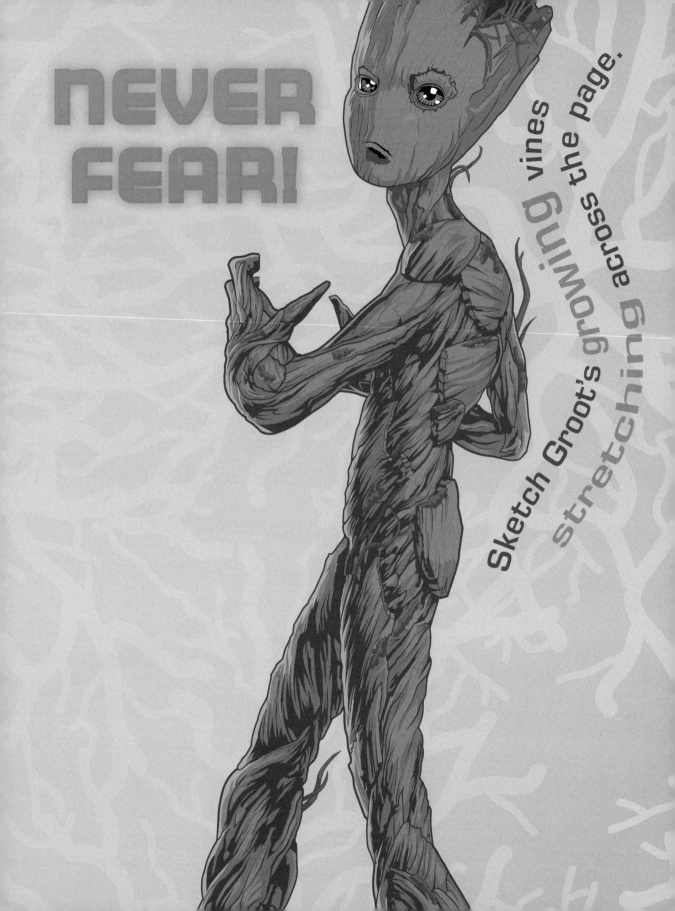

NEVER FEAR!

Sketch Groot's growing vines stretching across the page.

PICK AN AVENGER
TO BATTLE PROXIMA MIDNIGHT
AND THEN DRAW THE
FEARSOME
FIGHT SCENE.

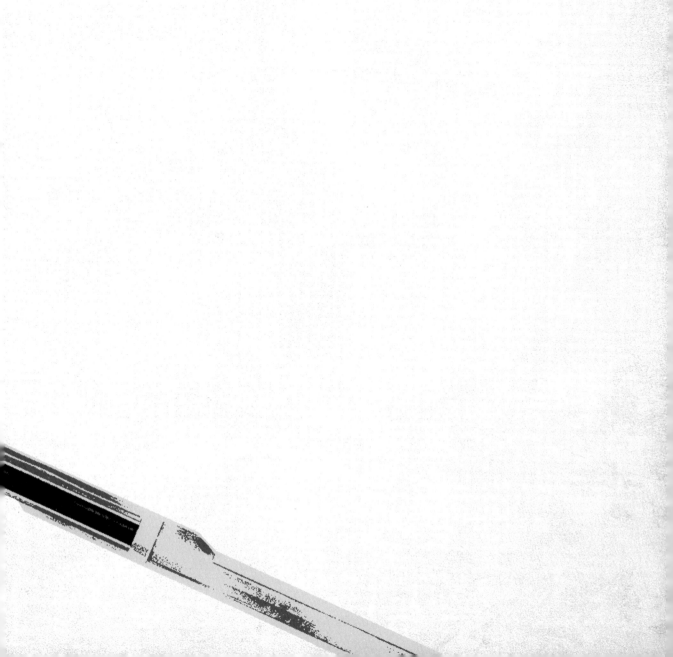

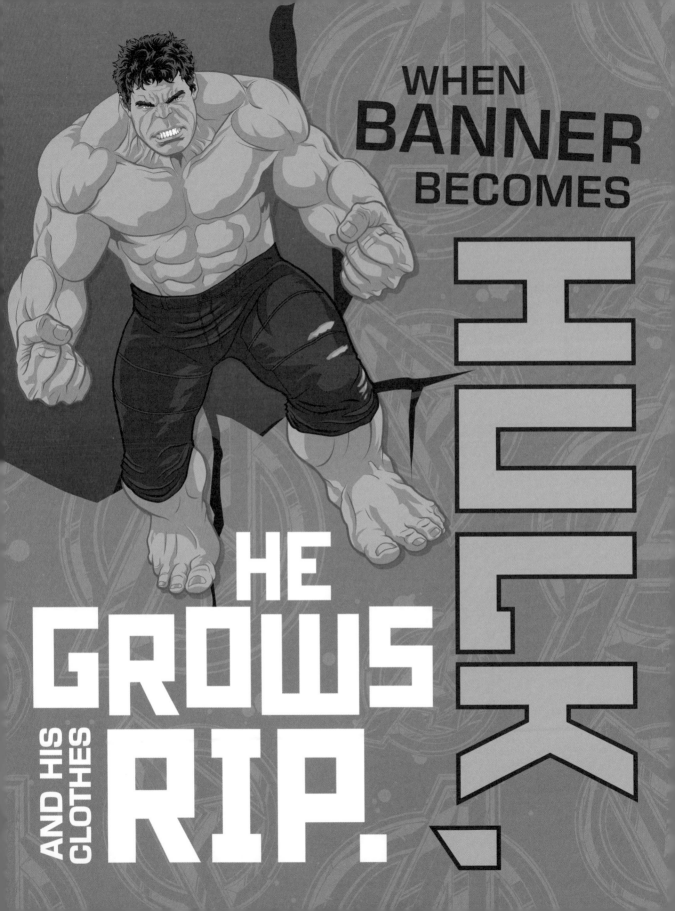

DESIGN A NEW OUTFIT FOR THE BIG GREEN GUY – IN EXTRA-LARGE SIZE!

DRAX'S BODY IS COVERED IN RED TATTOO-LIKE PATTERNS.

CREATE YOUR OWN UNIQUE DESIGNS. WHAT COLOUR WOULD YOU CHOOSE?

DESIGN A SECRET BASE FOR THE SUPER-SOLDIER SO THAT HE CAN REMAIN UNDER THE RADAR.

WHAT DO YOU THINK GROOT IS SAYING?

WRITE YOUR TRANSLATION IN EACH SPEECH BUBBLE.

"I AM GROOT"

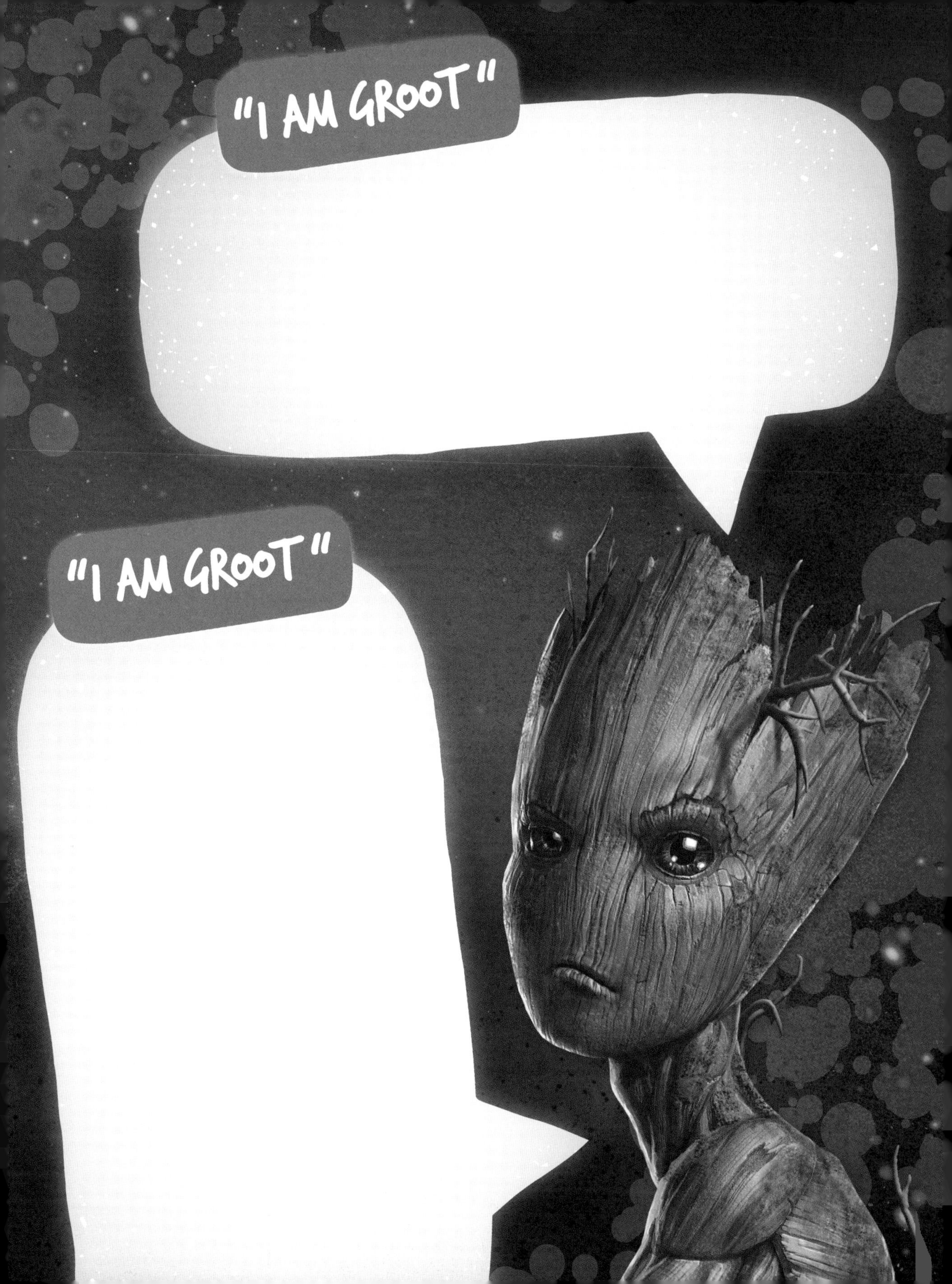
"I AM GROOT"
"I AM GROOT"

THE OUTRIDERS

ARE THANOS'S GENETICALLY ENGINEERED ARMY.

CREATE YOUR OWN ULTIMATE WARRIORS WITH UNIQUE WEAPONS.

UNIQUE WEAPONS

ADD **LEGS** TO EACH LITTLE CREATURE CRAWLING ACROSS THE PAGE.

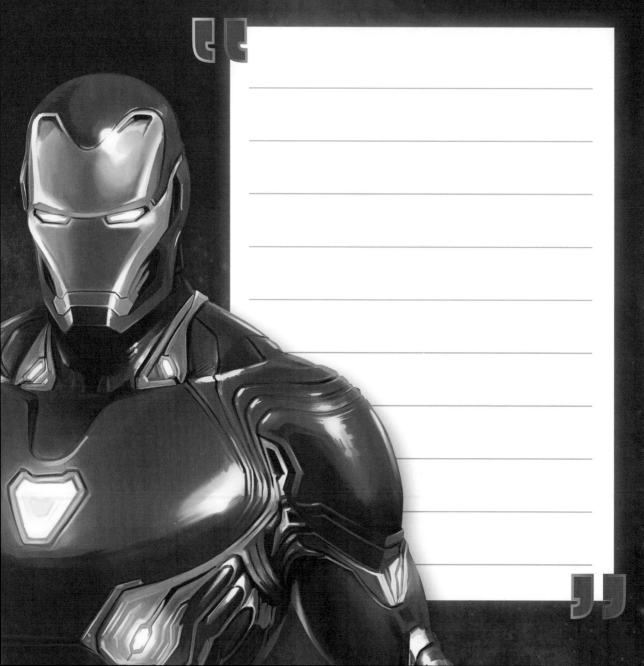

TONY STARK AND PETER QUILL

ARE BOTH FUNNY GUYS.

"

GIVE EACH OF THEM ONE OF YOUR BEST GAGS.

"

"

THE UNIVERSE IS
BIG!

DRAW A MAP OF IT – TO HELP THANOS WITH HIS SEARCH FOR THE INFINITY STONES.

THE AVENGERS ARE ALL SUPER HEROES.

SKETCH THE **MOST** HEROIC THING YOU'VE EVER **DONE** OR **SEEN.**

BLACK WIDOW
HAS GOT THE MOVES!

DRAW LOTS OF LASER BEAMS ACROSS THE PAGE FOR HER TO AVOID.

WAR MACHINE

WILL DO ANYTHING TO KEEP EARTH AND ITS PEOPLE SAFE FROM THE THREAT OF THANOS.

DRAW the planet Rhodey has vowed to protect.

With the AVENGERS, the GUARDIANS, DOCTOR STRANGE and IRON SPIDER all joining forces, they're going to need a bigger base.

DESIGN A BRAND-NEW HQ FOR THE HEROES.

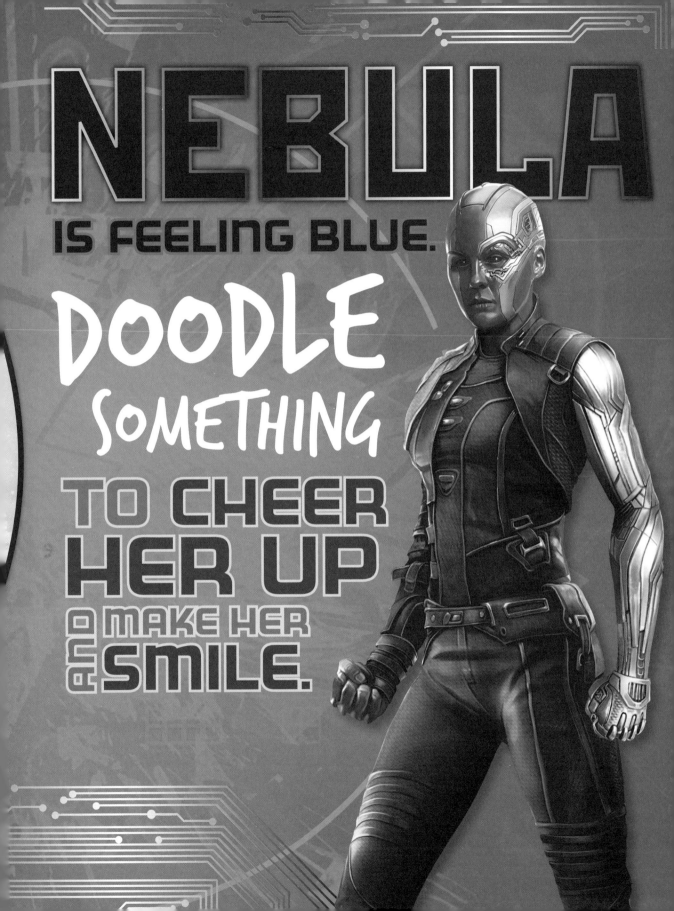

NEBULA

IS FEELING BLUE.

DOODLE SOMETHING

TO CHEER HER UP

and **MAKE HER SMILE.**

THANOS IS SEARCHING THE GALAXY FOR THE INFINITY STONES. THE GALAXY IS FULL OF SOME CRAZY-LOOKING CREATURES.

SKETCH SOME OF THEM HERE.

DRAW THEM HERE
IN A FEARSOME FIGHTING POSE.

STAR-LORD

HAS LENT HIS MUSIC TO ONE OF THE AVENGERS.

DRAW THE HERO HE'S SHARING HIS MUSIC WITH.

NOW THAT THEY'RE ALL WORKING TOGETHER,

CREATE AND COLOUR AN AWESOME NEW LOGO FOR THIS ULTIMATE TEAM OF SUPER HEROES.

THE INFINITY STONES

ARE HIDDEN ALL AROUND THE GALAXY.

LIST THE TOP TEN HIDING PLACES IN YOUR HOME.

1 ....

2 ....

3 ....

4 ....

5 ....

6 ....

7 ....

8 ....

9 ....

10 ....

ROCKET CAN BE A BIT OF A WISE GUY.

WRITE SOME SMART
COMMENTS AND WITTY
COMEBACKS FOR THE
GUARDIAN.

WHAT ARE THE SUPER HEROES LOOKING AT?

SKETCH SOMETHING ON THE TEAM'S BIG SCREEN.

DOCTOR STRANGE
CAN CONJURE UP A TIME-LOOP.

WHICH
MOMENT OF YOUR LIFE
WOULD YOU LIKE TO GO BACK TO
AGAIN AND AGAIN?

THE SUPER HEROES NEED FOOD TO FUEL THEM FOR THEIR MISSION.

DRAW A
DELICIOUS FEAST
FOR THE
GOOD GUYS
TO DEVOUR.

BLACK PANTHER

IS A SKILLED AND CUNNING WARRIOR.

DOODLE YOUR FAVOURITE BIG CAT BESIDE HIM.

WRITE A LETTER TO YOUR FAVOURITE SUPER HERO.
TELL THEM WHY YOU LOVE THEM!

DEAR _____

_____

_____

_____

_____

_____

_____

_____

_____

_____

LOVE FROM _____